My Country

CU00842231

My Country

by Queen of Rumania Marie

MY COUNTRY

The Queen of a small Country!

Those who are accustomed to see rulers of greater lands can little understand what it means.

It means work and anxiety and hope, and great toiling for small results. But the field is large, and, if the heart be willing, great is the work.

When young I thought it all work, uphill work; but the passing years brought another knowledge, a blessed knowledge, and now I know.

This is a small country, a new country, but it is a country I love. I want others to love it also; therefore listen to a few words about it. Let me paint a few pictures, draw a few sketches as I have seen them, first with my eyes, then with my heart.

*
**

Once I was a stranger to this people; now I am one of them, and, because I came from so far, better was I able to see them with their good qualities and with their defects.

Their country is a fruitful country, a country of vast plains, of waving corn, of deep forests, of rocky mountains, of rivers that in spring-time are turbulent with foaming waters, that in summer are but sluggish streams lost amongst stones. A country where peasants toil 'neath scorching suns, a country untouched by the squalor of manufactories, a country of extremes where the winters are icy and the summers burning hot.

A link between East and West.

At first it was an alien country, its roads too dusty, too endless its plains. I had to learn to see its beauties—to feel its needs with my heart.

Little by little the stranger became one of them, and now she would like the country of her birth to see this other country through the eyes of its Queen.

3

Yes, little by little I learnt to understand this people, and little by little it learned to understand me.

Now we trust each other, and so, if God wills, together we shall go towards a greater future!

My love of freedom and vast horizons, my love of open air and unexplored paths led to many a discovery. Alone I would ride for hours to reach a forlorn village, to see a crumbling church standing amongst its rustic crosses at a river's edge, or to be at a certain spot at sunset when sky and earth would be drenched with flaming red.

Oh! the Rumanian sunsets, how wondrous they are!

"THE THATCHED ROOFS ARE REPLACED BY ROOFS OF SHINGLE THAT SHINE IN THE SUN" (p. 13).

"VERY DIFFERENT ARE THE MOUNTAIN VILLAGES FROM THOSE OF THE PLAIN. THE COTTAGES ARE LESS MISERABLE"(p. 13).

"MANY A HEARTY WELCOME HAS BEEN GIVEN ME IN THESE LITTLE VILLAGES"(p. 13).

"SQUARE, HIGH BUILDINGS WITH AN OPEN GALLERY ROUND THE TOP"(p. 21).

Once I was riding slowly homewards.

The day had been torrid, the air was heavy with dust. In oceans of burnished gold the corn-fields spread before me. No breath of wind stirred their ripeness; they seemed waiting for the hour of harvest, proud of being the wealth of the land.

As far as my eye could reach, corn-fields, corn-fields, dwindling away towards the horizon in a vapoury line. A blue haze lay over the world, and with it a smell of dew and ripening seed was slowly rising out of the ground.

At the end of the road stood a well, its long pole like a giant finger pointing eternally to the sky. Beside it an old stone cross leaning on one side as though tired, a cross erected with the well in remembrance of some one who was dead....

Peace enveloped me—my horse made no movement, it also was under the evening spell.

From afar a herd of buffaloes came slowly towards me over the long straight road: an ungainly procession of beasts that might have belonged to antediluvian times.

One by one they advanced—mud-covered, patient, swinging their ugly bodies, carrying stiffly their heavily-horned heads, their vacant eyes staring at nothing, though here and there with raised faces they seemed to be seeking something from the skies.

From under their hoofs rose clouds of dust accompanying their every stride. The sinking sun caught hold of it, turning it into fiery smoke. It was as a veil of light spread over these beasts of burden, a glorious radiance advancing with them towards their rest.

I stood quite still and looked upon them as they passed me one by one.... And that evening a curtain seemed to have been drawn away from many a mystery. I had understood the meaning of the vast and fertile plain.

*

**

Twenty-three years have I now spent in this country, each day bringing its joy or its sorrow, its light or its shade; with each year my interests widened, my understanding deepened; I knew where I was needed to help.

I am not going to talk of my country's institutions, of its politics, of names known to the world. Others have done this more cleverly than I ever could. I want only to speak of its soul, of its atmosphere, of its peasants and soldiers, of things that made me love this country, that made my heart beat with its heart.

I have moved amongst the most humble. I have entered their cottages, asked them questions, taken their new-born in my arms.

I talked their language awkwardly, making many a mistake; but, although a stranger, nowhere amongst the peasants did I meet with distrust or suspicion. They were ready to converse with me, ready to let me enter their cottages, and especially ready to speak of their woes. It is always of their woes that the poor have to relate, but these did it with singular dignity, speaking of death and misery with stoic resignation, counting the graves of their children as another would count the trees planted round his house.

They are poor, they are ignorant, these peasants. They are neglected and superstitious, but there is a grand nobility in their race. They are frugal and sober, their wants are few, their desires limited; but one great dream each man cherishes in the depth of his heart: he wishes to be a landowner, to possess the ground that he tills; he wishes to call it his own. This they one and all told me; it was the monotonous refrain of all their talk.

*

**

When first I saw a Rumanian village, with its tiny huts hidden amongst trees, the only green spots on the immense plains, I could hardly believe that families could inhabit houses so small.

They resembled the houses we used to draw as children, with a door in the middle, a tiny window on each side, and smoke curling somewhere out of the heavily thatched roof. Often these roofs seem too heavy for the cottages; they seem to crush them, and the wide-open doors make them look as if they were screaming for help.

In the evening the women sit with their distaffs spinning on the doorsteps, whilst the herds come tramping home through the dust, and the dogs bark furiously, filling the air with their clamour.

Nowhere have I seen so many dogs as in a Rumanian village—a sore trial to the rider on a frisky horse.

All night long the dogs bark, answering each other. They are never still; it is a sound inseparable from the Rumanian night.

I always loved to wander through these villages. I have done so at each season, and every month has its charm.

In spring-time they are half-buried in fruit-trees, a foamy ocean of blossoms out of which the round roofs of the huts rise like large grey clouds.

Chickens, geese, and newly born pigs sport hither and thither over the doorsteps; early hyacinths and golden daffodils run loose in the untidy courtyards, where strangely shaped pots and bright rags of carpets lie about in picturesque disorder.

Amongst all this the half-naked black-eyed children crawl about in happy freedom.

"IT IS ESPECIALLY IN THE DOBRUDJA THAT THESE DIFFERENT NATIONALITIES JOSTLE TOGETHER" (p. 16).

Never was I able to understand how such large families, without counting fowls and many a four-footed friend, could find room in the two minute chambers of which these huts are composed.

In winter these villages are covered with snow; each hut is a white padded heap; all corners are rounded off so that every cottage has the aspect of being packed in cotton-wool.

No efforts are made to clear away the drifts. The snow lies there where it has fallen; the small sledges bump over its inequalities, forming roads as wavy as a storm-beaten sea!

The Rumanian peasant is never in a hurry. Time plays no part in his scheme of life. Accustomed to limitless horizons, he does not expect to reach the end of his way in a day.

In summer the carts, in winter the sledges, move along those endless roads, slowly, resignedly, with untiring patience.

Drawn by tiny, lean horses, the wooden sledges bump over the uneven snow, the peasant sits half-hidden amongst his stacks of wood, hay, or maize-stalks, according to the freight he may be transporting from place to place. Picturesque in his rough sheep-skin coat, he is just as picturesque in summer in his white shirt and broad felt hat, contentedly lying upon his stacked-up corn, whilst his long-suffering oxen trudge away, seemingly as indifferent as their master to the length of the road. They are stone-grey, these oxen-lean, strong, with large-spread horns; their eyes are beautiful, with almost human look.

The Rumanian road is a characteristic feature of the country. It is wide, it is dusty, generally it is straight, few trees shading its borders; mostly it is badly kept. But, like all things upon which civilisation has not yet laid too heavy a hand, it has an indefinite charm—the charm of immensity, something dreamy, something infinite, something that need never come to an end....

And along these roads the peasants' carts crawl, one after another in an endless file, enveloped in clouds of dust. If night overtake them on the way the oxen are unyoked, the carts are drawn up beside the ditch, till the rising dawn reminds them that there are still many miles to their goal....

When it rains the dust turns to mud; the road becomes then a river of mud!

Rumania is not a country of violent colours. There is a curious unity in its large horizons, its dusty roads, its white-clad peasants, its rough wooden carts. Even oxen and horses seem to have toned down to grey or dun, so as to become one with a sort of dreamy haziness that lies over the whole.

It is only the sunsets that turn all these shadowy tints into a sudden marvel of colour, flooding earth and sky with wondrous gold. I have seen hay-stacks change into fiery pyramids, rivers into burning ribbons, and pale, tired faces light up with a marvellous glow.

A fleeting hour this hour of sunset, but each time it bursts upon me as an eternally renewed promise sent by God above.

Perchance 'tis in winter and autumn that these sunsets are most glorious, when the earth is tired, when its year's labour is done, or when it is sleeping 'neath its shimmering shroud of snow, guarding in its bosom the harvest that is to come.

*
**

Very different are the mountain villages from those of the plain. The cottages are less miserable, less small, the thatched roofs are replaced by roofs of shingle that shine like silver in the sun. Richer and more varied are the peasants' costumes; the colours are brighter, and often a tiny flower-filled garden surrounds the house.

Autumn is the season to visit these villages amongst the hills; autumn, when the trees are a flaming glory, when the dying year sends out a last effort of beauty before being vanquished by frost and snow.

Many a hearty welcome has been given me in these little villages, the peasants receiving me with flower-filled hands. At the first sign of my carriage, troops of rustic riders gallop out to meet me, scampering helter-skelter on their shaggy little horses, bearing banners or flowering branches, shouting with delight. Full tilt they fly after my carriage, raising clouds of dust. Like their masters, the ponies are wild with excitement; all is noise, colour, movement; joy runs wild over the earth.

The bells of the village ring, their voices are full of gladness, they too cry out their welcome. Crowds of gaily clad women and children flock out of the houses, having plundered their gardens so as to strew flowers before the feet of their Queen.

The church generally stands in the middle of the village; here the sovereign must leave her carriage, and, surrounded by an eager, happy crowd, she is led towards the sanctuary, where the priest receives her at the door, cross in hand.

Wherever she moves the crowd moves with her; there is no awkwardness, no shyness, but neither is there any pushing or crushing. The Rumanian peasants remain dignified; they are seldom rowdy in their joy. They want to look at one, to touch one, to hear one's voice; but they show no astonishment and little curiosity. Mostly their expression remains serious, and their children stare at one with grave faces and huge, impressive eyes.

It is only the galloping riders who become loud in their joy.

"IT HAD KEPT THE DELIGHTFUL APPEARANCE OF HAVING BEEN MODELLED BY A POTTER'S THUMB" (p. 21).

"PRIMITIVE STRONGHOLDS, HALF TOWER, HALF PEASANT-HOUSE" (p. 21).

"RICHER AND MORE VARIED ARE THE PEASANTS' COSTUMES" (p. 13).

"WITH AN OPEN GALLERY ROUND THE TOP FORMED BY STOUT SHORT COLUMNS" (p. 21).

"COMPOSED OF A DOUBLE COLONNADE.... BEHIND THESE COLONNADES ARE THE NUNS' SMALL CELLS: TINY DOMES, LITTLE CHAMBERS" (p. 26).

There are some strange customs amongst the peasants, curious superstitions. Rumania being a dry country, it is lucky to arrive with rain: it means abundance, fertility, the hope of a fine harvest—wealth.

Sometimes as I went through the villages, the peasant women would put large wooden buckets full of water before their threshold; a full vessel is a sign of Good-luck. They will even sprinkle water before one's feet, always because of that strange superstition, that water is abundance, and, when the great one comes amongst them, honour must be done unto her in every way.

I have seen tall, handsome girls step out of their houses to meet me with overflowing water-jars on their heads; on my approach they stood quite still, the drops splashing over their faces so as well to prove that their pitchers were full.

It is lucky to meet a cart full of corn or straw coming towards one; but an empty cart is a sure sign of Ill-luck!

Many a time, in places I came to, the inhabitants have crowded around me, kissing my hands, the hem of my dress, falling down to kiss my feet, and more than once have they brought me their children, who made the Sign of the Cross before me as though I had been the holy Image in a church.

At first it was difficult unblushingly to accept such homage, but little by little I got accustomed to these loyal manifestations; half humble, half proud, I would advance amongst them, happy to be in their midst.

*

**

It were impossible to describe all I have seen, heard, or felt whilst moving amongst these simple, warm-hearted people; so many vivid pictures, so many touching scenes have remained imprinted on my heart. I have wandered through villages lost in forsaken spots, upon burning plains; I have climbed up to humble little houses clustering together on mountain-sides. I have come upon lovely little places hidden amongst giant pines. On forlorn seashores I have discovered humble hamlets where Turks dwelt in solitary aloofness; near the broad Danube I have strayed amongst tiny boroughs inhabited by Russian fisher-folk, whose type is so different from that of the Rumanian peasant. At first sight one recognises their nationality—tall, fair-bearded giants, with blue eyes, their red shirts visible from a great way off.

It is especially in the Dobrudja that these different nationalities jostle together: besides Rumanians, Bulgarians, Turks, Tartars, Russians, in places even Germans, live peacefully side by side.

I have been to a village in the Dobrudja which was part Rumanian, part Russian, part German, part Turkish. I went from one side to another, visiting many a cottage, entering each church, ending my round in the tiny rustic mosque hung with faded carpets, and there amongst a crowd of lowly Turks I listened to their curious service, of which I understood naught. A woman who is not veiled has no right to enter the holy precinct; but a royal name opens many a door, and many a severe rule is broken in the joy of receiving so unusual a guest.

On a burning summer's day I came to a tiny town almost entirely inhabited by Turks. I was distributing money amongst the poor and forsaken, and had been moving from place to place. Now it was the turn of the Mussulman population, therefore did I visit the most wretched quarters, my hands filled with many a coin.

Such was their joy at my coming that the real object of my visit was almost forgotten. I found myself surrounded by a swarm of excited women in strange attire, prattling a language I could not understand.

They called me Sultana, and each one wanted to touch me; they fingered my clothes, patted me on the back, one old hag even chucked me under the chin. They drew me with them from hut to hut, from court to court. I found myself separated from my companions, wandering in a world I had never known. Amongst a labyrinth of tiny mud-built huts, of ridiculously small gardens, of hidden little courts, did they drag me with them, making me enter their hovels, put my hand on their children, sit down on their stools. Like a swarm of crows they jabbered and fought over me, asking me questions, overwhelming me with kind wishes, to all of which I could answer but with a shrug of the shoulders and with smiles.

The poorer Mussulman women are not really veiled. They wear wide cotton trousers, and over these a sort of mantle which they hold together under the nose. The shape of these mantles gives them that indescribable line, so agreeable to the eye, and which alone belongs to the East. Also the colours they choose are always harmonious; besides, they are toned down to their surroundings by sun and dust. They wear strange dull blues and mauves—even their blacks are not really black, but have taken rusty tints that mingle pleasingly with the mud-coloured environment in which they dwell.

When attired for longer excursions, their garb is generally black, with a snow-white cloth on their heads, wrapped in such manner that it conceals the entire face, except the eyes.

Indescribably picturesque and mysterious are these dusky figures when they come towards one, grazing the walls, generally carrying a heavy staff in their hands; there is something biblical about them, something that takes one back to far-away times!

On this hot summer's morn of which I am relating, I managed to escape for a moment from my over-amiable assailants, so as to steal into a tiny hut of which the door stood wide open.

"A CONVENT ... WHITE AND LONELY, HIDDEN AWAY IN WOODED REGIONS GREENER AND SWEETER THAN ANY OTHER IN THE LAND" (p. 25).

Irresistibly attracted by its mysterious shade, I penetrated into the mud-made hovel, finding myself in almost complete darkness. At the farther end a wee window let in a small ray of light.

Groping my way, I came upon a pallet of rags, and upon that couch of misery I discovered an old, old woman—so old, so old, that she might have existed in the time of fairies and witches, times no more in touch with the bustle and noise of to-day.

Bending over her, I gazed into her shrunken face, and all the legends of my youth seemed to rise up before me, all the stories that as a child, entranced, I had listened to, stories one never forgets....

Above her, hanging from a rusty nail within reach of her hand, was a curiously shaped black earthenware pot. Everything around this old hag was the colour of the earth: her face, her dwelling, the rags that covered her, the floor on which I stood. The only touch of light in this hovel was a white lamb, crouching quite undisturbed at the foot of her bed.

Pressing some money between her crooked bony fingers, I left this strange old mortal to her snowy companion, and, stepping back into the sunshine, I had the sensation that for an instant it had been given me to stray through unnumbered ages into the days of yore.

From the beginning of time Rumania was a land subjected to invasions. One tyrannical master after another laid heavy hands upon its people; it was accustomed to be dominated, crushed, maltreated. Seldom was it allowed to affirm itself, to raise its head, to be independent, happy, or free; nevertheless, in spite of struggles and slavery, it was not a people destined to disappear. It overcame every hardship, stood every misery, endured every subjugation, could not be crushed out of being; but the result is that the Rumanian folk are not gay.

Their songs are sad, their dances slow, their amusements are seldom boisterous, rarely are their voices loud. On festive days they don their gayest apparel and, crowded together in the dust of the road, they will dance in groups or in wide circles, tirelessly, for many an hour; but even then they are not often joyful or loud, they are solemn and dignified, seeming to take their amusement demurely, without passion, without haste.

Their love-songs are long complaints; the tunes they play on their flutes wail out endlessly their longing and desire that appear to remain eternally unsatisfied, to contain no hope, no fulfilment.

For the same reason few very old houses exist; there is hardly a castle or a great monument remaining from out the past. What was the use of building fine habitations if any day the enemy might sweep over the country and burn everything to the ground?

One or two strange old constructions have been preserved from those times of invasion: square, high buildings with an open gallery round the top formed by stout short columns, and here and there, in the immense thickness of the walls, tiny windows as look-outs. Primitive strongholds, half tower, half peasant-house, they generally stand somewhat isolated and resemble nothing I have seen in other lands.

I have lived in one of these strange houses. The gallery, that once was a buttress, had been turned into a balcony, and from between the squat pillars a lovely view was to be had over hill and plain. The rooms beneath were small, low, irregular, behind great thick walls; a wooded staircase as steep as a ladder led to these chambers.

Both outside and inside the building was whitewashed, and so primitive was its construction, that it had kept the delightful appearance of having been modelled by a potter's thumb. There were no sharp angles, but something rounded and uneven about its corners that no modern dwelling can possess. The whole was crowned by a broad roof of shingle, grey, with silver lights.

But it is the old convents and monasteries of this country that have above all guarded treasure from out the past.

From the very first these secluded spots of beauty attracted me more than anything else; indescribable is the spell that they throw over me, almost inexplicable the delight with which they fill my soul!

As in many other countries, the Rumanian monks and nuns knew how to select the most enchanting places for their homes of peace.

I have wandered from one to another, discovering many a hidden treasure, visiting the richest and the poorest, those easy of access and those hidden away in mountain valleys, where the traveller's foot but rarely strays.

Some I was only able to reach on horseback, having climbed over hill and dale, up or down stony passes, followed by troops of white-clad peasants, mounted on shaggy, dishevelled ponies, sure-footed as mountain-goats.

Once at dusk, after a whole day's riding over the mountains, I came quite suddenly upon one of these far-away sanctuaries, whitewashed, strangely picturesque, half-hidden amongst pines and venerable beech-trees with trunks like giants turned suddenly to stone—giants that in their last agony are twisting their arms in useless despair.

On my approach the bells began ringing—their clear and strident voices proclaiming their joy to the skies.

I rode through the covered portal into the walled-in court. Before I could dismount I was surrounded by a dark swarm of nuns making humble gestures of greeting, crossing themselves, falling to their knees, and pressing their foreheads against the stones on the ground, catching hold of my hands or part of my garment, which they kissed, whilst they cried and murmured, mumbling many a prayer.

"THIS PORCH IS DECORATED ALL OVER WITH FRESCOES" (p. 26).

"SOME WERE SO OLD, SO BENT, THAT THEY COULD NO MORE RAISE THEIR HEADS TO LOOK UP AT THE SKY ABOVE" (p. 28).

"STRANGE OLD MONKS INHABITED IT" (p. 27).

"SILENT RECLUSES, BURIED AWAY FROM THE WORLD"
(p. 27).

Dazed by such a welcome, I was seized under the elbow by the
mother abbess, a venerable, tottering old woman, whose face was
seared by age as a field is furrowed by the plough.

Half leading me, half hanging on to me for support, she conducted me towards the open church-door. From time to time she would furtively kiss my shoulder, and in a sort of lowly ecstasy press her old, old face close to mine.

All the other nuns trooped after us like a flock of black-plumed birds, their dark veils waving about in the wind, the bells still ringing in peals of delight!

Within the dim sanctuary the lighted tapers were as swarms of fire-flies in a dusk-filled forest; the nuns grouped themselves along the walls, their dark dresses becoming one with the shadow, so that alone their faces stood out, rendered almost ethereal by the wavering candle-light.

They were chanting—fain would I say that their singing was beautiful, but that were scarcely the truth! Not as in Russia, the chanting in the Rumanian churches is far from melodious—they drone through the nose longdrawn, oft-repeated chants, anything but harmonious, and which seemingly have no reason ever to come to an end.

But somehow, that evening, in the forlorn mountain convent far from the homes of men, there, in the low-domed chapel, filled with those sable-clad figures whose earnest faces were almost angelic in the mystical light, the weird sounds that rose towards the roof were not out of place. There was something old-time about them, something archaic, primitive, in keeping with the somewhat barbaric paintings and images, something that seemed to have strayed down from past ages into the busier world of to-day....

More pompous were the receptions I received in the larger monasteries.

Here all the monks would file out to meet me—a procession of black-robed, long-bearded beings, austere of appearance, sombre of face.

Taking me by the arm, the Father Superior would solemnly lead me towards the gaily decorated church, whilst many little children would throw flowers before me as I passed.

Not over-severe are the monastic rules in Rumania. The convent-doors are open to all visitors; in former days they were houses of rest for travellers wandering from place to place.

Three days' hospitality did the holy walls offer to those passing that way; this was the ancient custom, and now in many places monks or nuns are allowed to let their little houses to those in need of a summer's rest. This, however, is only possible where the convents are real little villages, where more or less each recluse possesses his own small house.

There are two kinds of convents in this country: either a large building where all the monks or nuns are united beneath the same roof, or a quantity of tiny houses grouped in a large square round the central church.

The former alone are architecturally interesting, and some I have visited are exquisitely perfect in proportion and shape.

One of these convents above all others draws me towards it, for irresistible indeed is its charm.

A convent ... white and lonely, hidden away in wooded regions greener and sweeter than any other in the land. Perfect is the form of its church, snow-white the colonnades that surround its tranquil court. A charm and a mystery envelop it, such as nowhere else have I felt. Sober are its sculptures, but an indescribable harmony makes its lines beautiful, and such a peace pervades the place that here I felt as though I had truly found the house of rest....

Whenever I go there the nuns receive me with touching delight, half astonished that one so high should care about so simple a place. I go there often, whenever I can, for it has thrown a strange spell over me, and often again must I return to its whitewashed walls.

The building forms a quadrangle round the church, three sides of which are composed of a double colonnade, built one above the other, the upper one forming an open gallery running round the whole. Behind these colonnades are the nuns' small cells: tiny domes, little chambers, whitewashed, humble, and still....

Large is the church, noble of line, rich of sculpture, fronted by a large, covered porch supported by stone pillars richly carved. Like the interior of the building, this porch is decorated all over with frescoes, artless of conception, archaic of design, and harmonious, the colour having been toned down by the hand of time.

Within, the church is high, dim, mystical, entirely painted with strange-faced saints, who stare at one as though astonished to be disturbed out of their lonely silence and peace.

Many a treasure lies within these walls: ancient images, crumbling tombstones, a marvellously carved altar-screen, gilt and painted with incomparable skill, all the colours faded and blended together by the master of all arts—Time.

In shadowy corners, heavily chased lamps, hanging on chains from above, shed a mysterious light upon silver-framed icons, polished by many a pious kiss. In truth a holy sanctuary, inducing the spirit to soar above the things of this earth....

"AN INDESCRIBABLE HARMONY MAKES ITS LINES BEAUTIFUL" (p. 25).

The fourth side of the quadrangle is shut in by a high wall, with a door in the centre opening upon a narrow path that leads towards a second smaller temple, as perfect in shape as the greater building of the inner court. Here the nuns are buried; an idyllic spot enclosed by crumbling walls that wild rose-bushes, covered with delicate blooms, hold together by their long thorny arms. The strangely shaped wooden crosses that mark the graves stand amidst high, waving grass and venerable apple-trees that age seems to incline tenderly towards those slumbering beneath the sod at their feet.

All round—beech forests upon low, undulating hills; as background to these, mountains—blue, hazy, unreachable, forming a barrier against the outside world....

A place of beauty, a place of rest, a place of peace....

Many sites of beauty rise before my eyes when I think of these hidden houses of prayer. Countless is the number I have visited in all four corners of the land, and again I turn my feet towards them whenever I can.

Hard were it to say which are the more picturesque, the convents or the monasteries; both are equally interesting, equally quaint.

I remember a small monastery, nestling beneath the sides of a frowning mountain, surrounded by pine forests, dark and mysterious. The way leading there was tortuous, stony, difficult of access, yet the place itself was a small meadow-encircled paradise of tranquillity, green and reposeful as a dream of rest.

Strange old monks inhabited it—silent recluses, buried away from the world, shadowy spectres, almost sinister in their aloofness, their eyes having taken the look of forest-dwellers who are no more accustomed to look into the eyes of men.

Noiselessly they followed me wherever I went, heads bent, but their eyes watching me from beneath shaggy brows, their hands concealed within their wide hanging sleeves; it was as though dark shadows were dogging my every step.

I turned round and looked into their obscure faces—how far-away they seemed! Who were they? What was their story? what had been their childhood, their hopes, their loves? For the most part, I think, they were but humble, ignorant beings, with no wider ideals, no far-away visions of higher things. Some were so old, so bent that they could no more raise their heads to look up at the sky above; their long, grey beards had taken on the appearance of lichens growing upon fallen trees.

But one there was amongst them, tall and upright, with the pale, ascetic face of a saint. I know not his name, naught of his past; but he had a noble visage, and meseemed that in his eyes I could read dreams that were not only the dreams of this earth.

I cannot, alas! speak of all the convents I have seen, but one I must still mention, for indeed it is a rare little spot upon earth.

Hidden within the mouth of a cavern, lost in the wildest mountain region, there lies a tiny wee church, so small, so small that one must bend one's head to step over the threshold; it appears to be a toy, dropped there by some giant hand and forgotten. Only a tiny little wooden chapel guarded by a few hoary old monks, creatures so old and decrepit that they seem to have gathered moss like stones lying for ever in the same place....

No road leads to this sanctuary; one must seek one's way to it on foot or horseback, over mountain steeps and precipitous rocks. There it lies in the dark cave entry, solitary, grey, and ancient, like a hidden secret waiting to be found out.

Behind the wee church the hollow stretches, dark and tortuous, running in mysterious obscurity right into the heart of the earth. When the end is reached a gurgling of water is heard—a spring, ice-cold, bubbles there out of the earth, pure and fresh as the sources in the Garden of Eden....

I have known of passionate lovers coming to be married in this church, defying the hardships of the road, defying nature's frowning barriers, so as to be bound together for life in this far-away spot where crowds cannot gather.

On the way to this church, not far from the mouth of the cave, stands a lonely little cemetery, filled with crosses of wood. Here the monks who have lived out their solitary lives are finally laid to eternal rest. Dark are those crosses, standing like spectres against the naked rock. The summer suns scorch them, the winds of autumn beat them about, and ofttimes the snows of winter fell them to the ground. But in spring-time early crocuses and delicate anemones cluster around them, gathering in fragrant bunches about their feet.

Meseems that, in spite of its solitude, it would not be sad to be buried in such a spot....

*

**

Once I was riding through the melting snow. The road I was following, like all Rumanian roads, was long, long, endlessly long, dwindling away in the distance, becoming one with the colourless sky.

It was a day of depression, a day of thaw, when the world is at its worst.

All around me the flat plains lay waiting for something that did not come. The landscape appeared to be without horizon, to possess no frontiers: all was dully uniform, without life, without light, without joy. Silence lay over the earth—silence and dismal repose.

With loose reins and hanging heads my horse and I trudged along through the slush. We were going nowhere in particular; a sort of torpor of indifference had come over us, well in keeping with the melancholy of the day.

A damp fog hung like a faded veil close over the earth; it was not a dense fog, but wavered about like steam.

"A LONELY LITTLE CEMETERY, FILLED WITH CROSSES OF WOOD" (p. 29).

"ON LONELY MOUNTAIN-SIDES"(p. 29).

"GUARDED BY A FEW HOARY OLD MONKS" (p. 29).

"THERE LIES A TINY WEE CHURCHON LONELY
MOUNTAIN-SIDES" (p. 29).

"TALL AND UPRIGHT, WITH THE PALE, ASCETIC FACE OF A SAINT" (p. 28).

"CREATURES SO OLD AND DECREPIT THAT THEY SEEM TO HAVE GATHERED MOSS LIKE STONES LYING FOR EVER IN THE SAME PLACE" (p. 29).

"WHEN FOUND IN SUCH NUMBERS THEY ARE MOSTLY HEWN OUT OF WOOD" (p. 34).

"THESE STRANGE OLD CROSSES.... THEY STAND BY THE WAY-SIDE" (p. 33).

All of a sudden, I heard a weird sound coming towards me out of the distance, something the like of which I had never heard before....

Drawing in my reins, I stood still at the edge of the road wondering what I was to see.

Unexpected indeed was the procession that, like a strange dream, was coming towards me from out the mist!

Wading through the melting snow advanced two small boys, carrying between them a round tin platter on which lay a flat cake; behind them came an old priest carrying a cross in his hand, gaudily attired in faded finery—red, gold and blue. His heavy vestment was all splashed and soiled, his long hair and unkempt beard were dirty-grey, like the road upon which he walked. A sad old man, with no expression but that of misery upon his yellow shrunken face.

Close behind his heels followed a rough wooden cart drawn by oxen whose noses almost touched the ground; their breath formed small clouds about their heads, through which their eyes shone with patient anxiety.

It was from this cart that the weird sound was rising. What could it be? Then all at once I understood!

A plain deal coffin had been placed in the middle of the cart; seated around it were a number of old women, wailing and weeping, raising their voices in a dismal chant, that rang like a lament through the air. Their white hair was dishevelled, and their black veils floated around them like thin wisps of smoke.

Behind the cart walked four old gipsies playing doleful tunes upon their squeaky violins, whilst the women's voices took up the refrain in another key. Never had I heard dirge more mournful, nor more lugubrious a noise. Pressing after the gipsies came a knot of barefooted relatives, holding lighted tapers in their hands. The tiny flames looked almost ashamed of burning so dimly in the melancholy daylight.

In passing, these weary mortals raised pale faces, looking at me with mournful eyes that expressed no astonishment. Through the gloomy mist they appeared to be so many ghosts, come from nowhere, going towards I know not what. Like shadows they passed and were gone; ... but through the gathering fog the wailing came back to haunt me, curiously persistent, as though the dead from his narrow coffin were calling for help....

Long after this strange vision had disappeared, I stood gazing at the road where traces of their feet had remained imprinted upon the melted snow. Had it all been but an hallucination, created by the melancholy of the day?

As I turned my horse I was confronted by a shadow looming large at a little distance down the road. What could it be? Was this a day of weird apparitions?

It was not without difficulty that I induced my horse to approach the spot; verily, I think that sometimes horses see ghosts!...

On nearing, I perceived that what had frightened my mount was naught but a tall stone cross. Monumental, moss-grown, and mysterious, it stood all alone like a guardian keeping eternal watch over the road. From its outstretched arms great drops were falling to the ground like heavy tears....

Was the old cross weeping—weeping because a lovely funeral had passed that way?...

 *
**

I must talk a little about these strange old crosses that on all roads I have come upon, that I have met with in every part of the country.

As yet I have not quite fathomed their meaning—but I love them, they seem so well in keeping with the somewhat melancholy character of the land.

Generally they stand by the wayside, sometimes in stately solitude, sometimes in groups; sometimes they are of quaintly carved stone, sometimes they are of wood, crudely painted with figures of archaic saints.

No doubt these pious monuments have been raised to mark the places of some event; perhaps the death of some hero, or only the murder of a lonely traveller who was not destined to reach the end of his road....

Mostly they stand beside wells, bearing the names of those who, having thought of the thirsty, erected these watering-places in far-away spots.

Quaint of shape, they attract the eye from far; the peasant uncovers his head before them, murmuring a prayer for the dead.

At cross-roads I have sometimes come upon them ten in a row; when found in such numbers they are mostly hewn out of wood. Their forms and sizes are varied: some are immensely high and solid, covered by queer shingle roofs; often their design is intricate, several crosses, growing one out of another, forming a curious pattern, the whole painted in the crudest colours that sun and rain soon tone down to pleasant harmony.

Protected by their greater companions, many little crosses crowd alongside: round crosses and square crosses, crosses that are slim and upright, crosses that seem humbly to bend towards the ground....

On lonely roads these rustic testimonies of Faith are curiously fascinating. One wonders what vows were made when they were placed there by pious hands and believing hearts.

But, above all, the carved crosses of stone attract me. I have discovered them in all sorts of places; some are of rare beauty, covered with inscriptions entangled in wonderful designs.

"MOSTLY THEY STAND BESIDE WELLS" (p. 34).

I have come upon them on bare fields, on the edges of dusty roads, on the borders of dark forests, on lonely mountain-sides. I have found them on forsaken waters by the sea, where the gulls circled around them caressing them gently with the tips of their wings.

Many a mile have I ridden so as to have another look at these mysterious symbols, for always anew they fill my soul with an intense desire for tranquillity; they are so solemnly impressive, so silent, so still....

One especially was dear to my heart. It stood all alone in dignified solitude upon a barren field, frowning down upon a tangle of thistles that twisted their thorny stems beneath the shade of its arms.

I know not its history, nor why it was watching over so lonely a place; it appeared to have been there from the beginning of time. Tired of its useless vigil, it was leaning slightly on one side, and at dusk its shadow strangely resembled the shadow of a man.

*

**

Nothing is more touchingly picturesque than the village cemeteries: the humbler they are the more do they delight the artist's eye.

Often they are placed round the village church, but sometimes they lie quite apart. I always seek them out, loving to wander through their poetical desolation—feeling so far, so far from the noise and haste of our turbulent world.

Certainly these little burial-grounds are not tended and cared for as in tidier lands. The graves are scattered about amidst weeds and nettles, sometimes thistles grow so thickly about the crosses that they half hide them from sight. But in spring-time, before the grass is high, I have found some of them nearly buried in daffodils and irises running riot all over the place. The shadowy crosses look down upon all that wealth of colour as though wondering if God Himself had adorned their forsaken graves.

The Rumanian peasant is averse from any unnecessary effort. What must happen happens, what must fall falls. Therefore, if a cross is broken, why try to set it up again?—let it lie! the grass will cover it, the flowers will cluster in its place.

On Good Friday morning I was roaming through one of these village churchyards. To my astonishment I found that nearly every grave was lighted with a tiny thin taper, the flame of which burnt palely, incapable of vying with the light of the sun. Lying beside these ghostly little lights were broken fragments of pottery filled with smouldering ashes, that sent thin spirals of blue smoke into the tranquil spring air. On this day of mourning the living come to do honour to their dead according to their customs, according to their Faith.

A strange sight indeed! all those wavering little flames amongst the crumbling graves. Often did I find a candle standing on a spot where all vestige of the grave itself had been entirely effaced; but it stood there burning bravely—some one remembering that just beneath that very inch of ground a heart had been laid to rest.

An old woman I found that morning standing quite still beside one of those tapers—a taper so humble and thin that it could scarcely remain upright—but with crossed arms the old mother was watching it, as though silently accomplishing some rite.

Approaching her, I looked to see of what size was the grave she was guarding, but could perceive no grave at all! The yellow little taper was humbly standing beside a bunch of anemones. All that once had been a tomb had long since been trodden into the ground.

The cloth round the old woman's head was white, white as the blossoming cherry-trees that made gay this little garden of God; white were also the flowers that grew beside the old woman's offering of love.

"Who is buried there?" I asked.

"One of my own," was her answer. "She was my daughter's little daughter; now she is at rest."

"Why is the grave no more to be seen?" was my next inquiry.

For all answer a shrug of the shoulders, and the dim eyes looked into mine; complete resignation was what I read in their depths.

"What is the use of keeping a grave tidy if the priest of the village allows his oxen to graze about amidst the tombs?"

I looked at her in astonishment. "Could not such disorder be put a stop to?"

Again a shrug of the shoulders. "Who is there to put a stop to it? The cattle must have somewhere to feed!"

I saw that she considered it quite natural, and that which lay beneath the ground could verily be indifferent to those passing hoofs, as long as on Good Friday some one remembered to burn a taper over her heart!

On Good Friday night, long services are celebrated in every church or chapel in the land.

Full of mystical charm are those peasant gatherings round their humble houses of prayer. Men, women, and children flock together, each one bearing a light. Those who find no place within stand outside in patient crowds.

A lovely picture indeed.

From each church window the light streams forth, whilst weird chants float out to those waiting beyond. In front of the sanctuary hundreds of wavering little flames, lighting up the visages of those who, with ecstatic faces, are hearkening for sounds of the service that is being celebrated within.

Custom will have it that, on Good Friday nights, flowers shall be brought by the worshippers—flowers that are reverently laid upon an embroidered effigy of the crucified Christ which is placed on a table in the centre of the church.

"QUAINT OF SHAPE, THEY ATTRACT THE EYE FROM FAR" (p. 34).

"SOMETIMES THEY ARE OF QUAINTLY CARVED STONE" (p. 33).

"STRANGE OLD CROSSES THAT ON ALL ROADS I HAVE COME UPON" (p. 33).

"THEIR FORMS AND SIZES ARE VARIED" (p. 34).

"NONE OF THE GREATER BUILDINGS ATTRACT ME SO STRONGLY AS THOSE LITTLE VILLAGE CHURCHES" (p. 40).

"THE ALTAR IS SHUT OFF FROM THE REST OF THE
BUILDING BY A CARVED AND PAINTED SCREEN" (p. 42).

Each believer brings what he can: a scrap of green, a branch of
blossoms, a handful of hyacinths, making the night sweet with
their perfume, or a bunch of simple violets gathered along the
wayside—first dear messengers of spring.

When the service is over, in long processions the worshippers
return to their homes, one and all carefully shading the tapers, for it
is lucky to bring them lighted back to the house.

No more light shines now from the church windows; all is swathed in darkness; the church itself stands out a huge mass of shade against the sky.

But the graveyard beyond is a garden of light! Have all the stars fallen from the heavens to console those lying beneath the sod? or is it only the tiny tapers still bravely burning, burning for the dead?...

*

**

There are some wonderful old churches in the country, stately buildings, rich and venerable, full of treasures carefully preserved from out the past.

I have visited all these churches, inquiring into their history, admiring their perfect proportions, closely examining their costly embroideries, their carvings, their silver lamps, their enamelled crosses, their Bibles bound in gold.

But, in spite of their beauty, none of the greater buildings attract me so strongly as those little village churches I have hunted up in the far-away corners of the land.

One part of the country is especially rich in these quaint little buildings: it is a part I dearly love. No railway desecrates its tranquil valleys, no modern improvement has destroyed its simple charm. Here the hand of civilisation has marred no original beauty; no well-meaning painter has touched up the faded frescoes on ancient walls. A corner of the earth that has preserved its personality; being difficult to reach, it has remained unchanged, unspoilt.

The axe has not felled its glorious forests, the enterprising speculator has built no hideous hotels, no places of entertainment; no monstrous advertisements disfigure its green meadows, its fertile inclines.

Therefore, also, have the tiniest little churches been preserved. They lie scattered about in quite unlikely places; perched on steep hill-tops, hidden in wooded valleys, often reflecting their quaint silhouettes in rivers flowing at their base.

Seen from afar, tall fir-trees, planted like sentinels before their porches, are the sign-posts marking the sites where they stand. The churches behind are so diminutive that from a distance the trees alone are to be seen.

These fir-trees seemed to beckon to me, promising that I should find treasures hidden at their feet—they stand out darkly distinct in the landscape, for it is a region where the forests are of beeches, not of pines.

Often I wandered miles to reach them, over stony paths, over muddy ground, through turbulent little streams and endless inclines, and never was I disappointed; the dark sentinels never called me in vain. The most lovely little buildings have I discovered in these far-away places.

Some were all of wood, warm in colour, like newly baked brown bread, their enormous roofs giving them the appearance of giant mushrooms growing in fertile ground.

There is generally a belfry on the top, but with some the belfry stands by itself in front of the church, and is mostly deliciously quaint of shape.

Indescribable is the colour the old wood takes on. It is always in harmony with its background, with its surroundings; be it on a green meadow, or against dark pines, be it in spring-time half concealed behind apple-trees in full bloom, be it in autumn when the trees that enclose it are all golden and russet and red.

The wood is dark-brown, with grey lights that are sometimes silver. Green moss often pads the chinks between the beams, giving the whole a soft velvety appearance that satisfies the eye.

Within, these rustic sanctuaries are toy copies of larger models; everything is tiny, but disposed in the same way. In orthodox churches the altar is shut off from the rest of the building by a carved and painted screen that nearly touches the roof, and is generally crowned by an enormous cross. At the lower part of these separations are the pictures of the most venerated saints. There are three small doors in these screens; during part of the service these doors remain closed.

Women have no right to penetrate within the Holy of Holies behind the screen.

Beautiful icons have I sometimes found in these forsaken little churches, carried there no doubt from greater ones when so-called improvements banished from their renovated walls the old-time treasures forthwith considered too shabby or too defaced.

Well do I remember one evening, after having climbed an endless way, I came at last to the foot of the pine-trees that had beckoned to me from afar, and how I reached the open door of the sanctuary at the very moment when the sun was going down.

The day had been wet, but this last hour before dusk was trying by its beauty to make up for earlier frowns.

The villagers, having guessed my intentions, had sent an old peasant to open the church. As I approached, the sound of a bell reached me, tolling its greeting into the evening air.

"THE ROOFS ARE ALWAYS OF SHINGLE" (p. <u>44</u>).

The last rays of the sun were lying golden on the building as I reached the door. Like dancing flames they had penetrated inside, spreading their glorious light over the humble interior, surrounding the saints' painted effigies with luminous haloes.

It was a wondrous sight!

On the threshold stood an old peasant, all in white, his hands full of flowering cherry-branches, which he offered me as he bent down to kiss the hem of my gown.

Within, the old man's loving fingers had lit many lights, and the same blossoms had been piously laid around the holiest of the icons, the one that each believer must kiss on entering the church.

The sunlight outshone the little tapers, but they seemed to promise to continue its glory to the best of their ability when the great parent should have gone to rest.... Sitting down in a shadowy corner, I let the marvellous peace of the place penetrate my soul, let the charm of this holy house envelop me like a veil of rest.

The sun had disappeared; now the little lights stood out, sharp points of brightness against the invading dusk.

Hard it was indeed to tear myself away; but time, being no respecter of human emotions, moves on!

Outside the door an enormous stone cross stood like a ghost, its head lost amongst the snowy branches of a tree in full bloom. This cross was almost as high as the church....

Varied indeed are the shapes of these peasant churches. When they are not of wood, like those I have just described, they are mostly whitewashed, their principal feature being the stout columns that support the porch in front. There is hardly a Rumanian church without this front porch; it gives character to the whole; it is the principal source of decoration. Sometimes the columns have beautiful carved capitals of rarest design; sometimes they are but solid pillars, whitewashed like the rest of the church.

Quaint indeed are the buildings that some simple-hearted artist has painted all over with emaciated, brightly robed saints. I have seen the strangest decorations of this sort: whole processions of archaic figures in stiff attitudes illustrating events out of their holy lives. Then the front columns are also painted, often with quite lovely designs, closely resembling Persian patterns in old blues and reds and browns.

The roofs are always of shingle, with broad advancing eaves of most characteristic shape.

A church have I seen in the middle of a maize field. The roof had fallen in, the walls were cracked, in places crumbling away, tall sunflowers peeped in at its paneless windows, and the birds built their nests amongst the beams of its ruined vaults. Pitiable it was, indeed, to contemplate such desolation; yet never had I seen a more magical sight.

The walls were still covered with frescoes, the colours almost unspoilt; the richly carved altar-screen still showed signs of gilding; hardly defaced were its many little pictures of saints. The stalwart pillars separating one part from the other stood strong and untouched except that in parts their plaster coating had crumbled away.

Quite unique was the charm of that ruin. The blue sky above was its roof, and the solemn saints stared down from the walls as if demanding why no kindly hand was raised to protect their fragile beauty from storm and rain.

I know not why such a treasure was allowed to fall to pieces— perchance there is no time to look after old ruins in a country where so much has still to be done! Indeed, the church was rarely fascinating, thus exposed to the light of the day, yet distressing was the thought that, if not soon covered in, the lovely frescoes would entirely fall away.

There was a figure of the Holy Virgin that especially attracted my attention; she stared at me from her golden background with large, pathetic eyes. Upon her knees the Child Christ sat, stiffly upright, one hand raised in blessing; the child was tiny, with a strange pale countenance and eyes much too large for its face.

I could not tear myself away from this forsaken place of prayer; again and again I made the round of it, absorbing into my soul the picture it made.

At last I left it, but many times did I turn round to have a last look.

The sunflowers stood in tall groups, their heads bent towards the church as though trying to look inside; a flight of snow-white doves circled about it, their spotless wings flashing in the light. It was the last I saw of it—the ruined walls, and, floating above them, those snow-white doves.

   *

  **

Much more would I delight to relate about these little churches. For me the topic is full of unending charm; but there are many things that I must still talk about, so regretfully I turn away to other scenes.

The most lonely inhabitants of Rumania are the shepherds—more lonely even than the monks in their cells, for the monks are gathered together in congregations, whilst the shepherds spend whole months alone with their dogs upon desolate mountain-tops.

Often when roaming on horseback on the summits have I come upon these silent watchers leaning on their staffs, standing so still that they might have been figures carved out of stone.

"VARIED INDEED ARE THE SHAPES OF THESE PEASANT CHURCHES" (p. 44).

"THEIR PRINCIPAL FEATURE BEING THE STOUT COLUMNS THAT SUPPORT THE PORCH IN FRONT" (p. 44).

"BUT WITH SOME THE BELFRY STANDS BY ITSELF" (p. 41).

"THE COLUMNS HAVE BEAUTIFUL CARVED CAPITALS OF RAREST DESIGN ... WHITEWASHED LIKE THE REST OF THE CHURCH (p. 44).

"QUAINT INDEED ARE THE BUILDINGS THAT SOME SIMPLE-HEARTED ARTIST HAS PAINTED" (p. 44).

The great blue sky was theirs, and the marvellous view over limitless horizons; theirs were the shifting clouds, floating sometimes above their heads, sometimes rising like steam out of the chasms at their feet; theirs were also the silence and the sunsets, the sunrise and the little mountain flowers with their marvellous tints. But also the storm was theirs, and the rain, and the days of impenetrable mist; theirs was the wordless solitude unrelieved by human voice.

These lonely mountain-dwellers become almost one in colour with the rocks and earth by which they are surrounded.

Enormous mantles do they wear, made of skins taken from sheep of their flock, fallen by the way. These shaggy garments give them a wild appearance resembling nothing I have ever seen; even tiny boys wear these extraordinary coats that cover them from head to foot, sheltering them from rain and storm, and even from the too ardent rays of the sun. Their only refuges are dug-outs, half beneath the earth, of which the roofs are covered with turf, so that even at a short distance they can hardly be seen. Here, in company with their dogs, they spend the long summer months, till the frosts of autumn send them and their flocks back to the plains.

Fierce-looking creatures are these shepherds, almost as unkempt as their dogs. Solitude seems to have crept into their eyes, that look at you without sympathy, as though they had lost the habit of focusing them to the faces of men.

A sore danger to the wanderer are those savage dogs, and often will their masters look on at the attacks they make upon the unfortunate intruder, without moving a finger in his defence.

No doubt sometimes a poet's soul is to be found amongst these highland-watchers. He will then tell tales worth listening to, for Nature will have been his teacher, the voices of the wilds have entered his heart.

Less unsociable is the shepherd tending his flock in greener pastures. He is less lonely; even when not living with a companion he receives the visits of passers-by—his expression is less grim, his eyes less hard, and the tunes he plays on his flute have a softer note.

Here the great-coat is discarded, but the "cioban's" attitude is always the same: be he on bare mountain pinnacles, or on juicy pastures near clear-flowing stream, or on the burning plains of the Dobrudja where for miles around no tree is to be seen, the "cioban" stands, for hours at a time, both hands under his chin, leaning on his staff. He keeps no record of time; he stares before him, and slowly the hours pass over his head.

Once I had a curious impression. I was riding over some endless downs near the sea. Nothing could be flatter than the landscape that stretched before me; the sea was a dead calm, resembling a mirror of spangled blue; the sand was white and dazzling; waves of heat rose from the ground, scorching my face; the entire world seemed to be gasping for breath. I alone was moving upon this immensity; sky, sea, and sand belonged to me.

In spite of the suffocating temperature, my horse was galloping briskly, happy to feel the soft sand beneath his hoofs. I had the sensation of moving through the desert.

All at once the animal became restive; he snorted through dilated nostrils, I felt him tremble beneath me; sweat broke out all over his body; suddenly he stopped short, and, swerving round unexpectedly, refused to advance! Nothing was to be seen but a series of flat, curving sand-hills, with here and there a tuft of hard grass, or sprays of sea-lavender, bending beneath the overpowering heat, yet I also had an uncanny sensation, the curious feeling that something was breathing, as though the ground itself were throbbing beneath our feet. In a way I shared my horse's apprehension. What could it be?

In spite of his reluctance, I pushed him forward, keeping a firm grip on the reins, as at each moment he tried to swing round.

Then I saw something strange appear on the horizon; a mysterious line undulating across one of the mounds, something that was alive. I had the keen perception that it was breathing, that it was even gasping for breath.

All at once a man rose from somewhere and stood, a dark splotch, against the brooding heat of the sky. The man was a shepherd! Then I understood the meaning of that weirdly palpitating line—it was his flock of sheep!

Stifled by the overwhelming temperature, they had massed themselves together, heads turned inwards, seeking shelter one from the other. Finding no relief, they were panting out their silent distress.

The "cioban" stood quite still, staring at me with stupefied indifference.

I think that never before and never since have I had an acuter sensation of intolerable heat....

Wherever I have met them, be it on the mountains or in the plains, on green pastures or on arid wastes, these silent shepherds have seemed to me the very personification of solitude, of mystery, of things unsaid.

Because of their lonely vigils amongst voiceless wilds, they have surely returned to a nearer comprehension of nature; perchance they have discovered strange secrets that none of us know!

In autumn and early spring the shepherds lead their flocks back from the mountains. One meets them trudging slowly along the high-roads—a silent mass with a weather-beaten leader at their head, man and beast the colour of dust; foot-sore, weary, passive, knowing that their way is not yet at an end.

"THESE LONELY MOUNTAIN-DWELLERS" (p. 47).

Fleeting visions of the wilds, wraiths come back from solitudes of which we know naught. The men with brooding faces and far-seeing eyes, the animals with hanging heads, come towards one out of the distance, pass, move away, and are gone ... leaving behind them on the road thousands and thousands of tiny traces that wind or rain soon efface....

 *
**

There is a wandering people known in every land—a people surrounded by mystery, whose origin has never been clearly established, a people that even in our days are nomads, moving, always moving from place to place. Wherever they stray, the gipsies are looked upon with mistrust and suspicion; they are known to be thieves; their dark faces and flashing teeth at once attract and repel. There is a nameless charm about them, and yet aliens they are wherever they go. Every man's hand is against them; nowhere are they welcome, ever must they move on and on homeless, despised, and restless, wanderers indeed on the face of the earth.

Yet there are places in Rumania where those gipsies have settled down on the outskirts of villages or towns.

There, in the midst of indescribable filth and disorder, they are massed together in tumble-down huts and dug-outs, half-naked, surrounded by squabbling children and savage dogs. Their hovels are covered with whatever they can lay hand upon: old tins, broken boards, rags, clods of earth, torn strips of carpets; no words can render the squalor that surrounds them, the abject misery in which they swarm.

I have never been able to discover if always the same gipsies live in these places, or if, after a time, they move on, leaving their nameless hovels to other wanderers, who for a time settle down and then depart, making place for those who still will come.

I am inclined to think that in some cases these settlements are refuges where the wandering hordes seek shelter in winter, when snow-drifts and bitter frosts make the high-roads impracticable. Yet also in summer have I seen families grovelling about in these sordid suburbs.

Infinitely more picturesque are the gipsy-camps. These strange people will pitch their tents in all sorts of places. On large fields used for pasture, on the edge of streams, sometimes on islands in the midst of river-beds, or on the border of woods.

Along the road they come, not in covered vans as we see them in tamer countries, but in dilapidated carts, drawn by lean, half-starved horses, sometimes by mules or patient grey donkeys.

On these carts, amidst an indescribable jumble of poles, carpets, tent-covers, pots, pans, and other implements, whole families find place—mothers and children, old grannies and greybeards, little boys and bigger youths, regardless of the unfortunate animals that half succumb beneath the burden.

They stop where they can, sometimes where they must—for many places are prohibited, and no one desires to have the thieving rascals too near their home.

To me these camps have always been an unending source of interest. Whenever, from afar, I have perceived the silhouettes of gipsy-tents, I have never failed to go there, and no end of impressions have I gathered amongst these wandering aliens. Often have I watched the carts being unloaded; with much noise and strife the tent-poles are fixed in the ground, discoloured rags of every description are spread over them, each family erecting the roof beneath which it will shelter for awhile its eternal unrest.

Many and many a time have I roamed about amidst the tents of these jabbering, squabbling hordes of beggars, beset by hundreds of brown hands asking for pennies, surrounded by dark faces with brilliant eyes and snow-white teeth. Half cringing, half haughty, they would demand money, laughing the while and shrugging their shoulders, fingering my clothes, slipping their fingers into my pockets; sometimes I have almost had the sensation of being assailed by a troop of apes.

When on horseback they have nearly pulled me from the saddle, overwhelming me with strange blessings that often sounded more like curses or imprecations.

But one wish that they cried after me was always gratefully accepted by my heart; it was the wish of "Good luck" to my horse. Being nomads, they appreciate the value of a good mount, and as from all time my horse has been my friend, such an invocation could not leave me unmoved; on those days, the pennies I scattered amongst them were given with a readier hand.

The most beautiful types have I discovered amongst these people; at all ages they are inconceivably picturesque, so much so indeed that occasionally they seemed to have got themselves up with a view to effect.

Old hags have I seen crouching beneath their tents, bending over steaming pots, stirring mysterious messes with pieces of broken sticks. No old witch out of Andersen's fairy-tales or the "Arabian Nights" could be compared to these weird old beings draped in faded rags that once had been bright, but that now were as sordid and ancient as the old creatures they only half clothed.

Gaudy bands of stuff were wound turban-wise round their heads, from beneath which strands of grey hair hung in dishevelled disorder over their eyes. Generally a white-clay pipe was stuck in the corner of their mouths, for both the men and women smoke; in fact, smoke pervades the atmosphere about them, fumes of tobacco mixing with the more pungent smell of the fires lighted all over the camp.

"THESE SHAGGY GARMENTS GIVE THEM A WILD APPEARANCE" (p. 47).

"THEIR ONLY REFUGES ARE DUG-OUTS" (p. <u>47</u>).

"EVEN TINY BOYS WEAR THESE EXTRAORDINARY COATS" (p. 47).

"HERE, IN COMPANY WITH THEIR DOGS, THEY SPEND THE LONG SUMMER MONTHS" (p. 47).

"ON JUICY PASTURES NEAR CLEAR-FLOWING STREAM" (p. 48).

"SILENT WATCHERS LEANING ON THEIR STAFFS" (p. 46).

"WHEREVER I HAVE MET THEM, BE IT ON THE MOUNTAINS OR IN THE PLAINS, ... THESE SILENT SHEPHERDS HAVE SEEMED TO ME THE VERY PERSONIFICATION OF SOLITUDE" (p. 50).

These old crones are the respected members of the tribes. Their loud curses call order to the young ones, throw a certain awe amongst the rowdy quarrelling children, who run about almost naked clamouring for alms, turning summersaults in the dust, tumbling about between one's feet. A sore trial to one's patience are these scamps, but at the same time a source of infinite delight to the eye, for extraordinarily beautiful are some of these grinning, screeching little savages, one with the colour of the earth; small bronze statues with curly, tousled heads, large eyes bordered by indescribable lashes, sometimes so long and curling that they appear to be black feathers at their lids.

Occasionally a torn shirt barely covers them, or their arms have been thrust into coats much too large, the sleeves dangling limply over their hands, giving them the appearance of small scarecrows come to life. Never more enchanting are they than when gambolling about as God made them, for all attire a string of bright beads round their necks!

These earth-coloured little waifs will run for miles beside one's carriage or horse, begging for coins with extended palms, whining over and over again the same complaint.

Most beautiful of all are the young girls: upright, well grown, with narrow hips and delicate hands and feet. Whatever rag they twist about their graceful limbs turns into a becoming apparel. They will deck themselves with any discarded finery they may pick up by the way. Sometimes valuable old pieces of embroidery will end their days upon the bodies of these attractive creatures, enhancing their charm, giving them the air of beggared queens. Bright girdles wound round hips and waist keep all these rags in place, giving the wearer the look of Egyptians such as we see painted on the frescoes of temple-walls.

Beneath the gaudy scarves which they tie on their heads plaits of hair hang down on both sides of their faces—plaits that are decorated with every sort of coin, with little splinters of coloured glass or metal, or strange-shaped charms or holy medals that jingle as they move about. Round their necks hang long strings of gaudy beads that shine and glisten on their bronze-tinted skins.

Little modesty do these maidens show. They are loud and forward, shameless beggars, quite indifferent if their torn shirts leave neck and bosom half naked to the rays of the sun.

With flashing white teeth they will smile at you, arms akimbo, head thrown back, a white pipe impudently stuck at the corner of their mouths.

Indescribably graceful are these girls coming back to the camp at evening, carrying large wooden water-pots on their heads. Over the distance they advance, upright, with swinging stride, whilst the water splashes in large drops over their cheeks. The sinking sun behind them gives them the appearance of shadows coming from very far out of the desert where the paths have neither beginning nor end....

The men are no less picturesque than the women; they are covered with filthy rags, and are mostly barefooted. But tribes have I encountered less sordid, where the men wore high boots, baggy trousers, and shirts with wide-hanging sleeves. These belonged to more prosperous clans, the men particularly good-looking, with long curling hair hanging on both sides of their faces. Evil-looking creatures no doubt, but uncannily handsome nevertheless.

Most gipsies are tinkers by profession, by instinct they are thieves. Leaving their women-folk to look after the tents, the men will set out towards the villages, there to patch up pots and pans; often one meets them several in file carrying bright copper vessels on their backs. They grin at you, and never forget to stretch out a begging hand.

Others have studied the gipsies' habits, morals, and ways; I have only looked upon them with an artist's eye, and in that way they are an unending source of joy.

Inconceivable is the bustle and noise when a camp breaks up. The tent-poles are pulled out of the ground, the miserable horses that have been seeking scarce nourishment from the withered wayside grass are caught by the screeching children, who have easy work, as the unfortunate creatures are hobbled and cannot escape. Resignedly they let themselves be attached to the carts, the tent-poles, carpets, pots and pans are once more transferred from the ground to the vehicles that will transport them to another place, and thus onwards ... without end....

The old crones are stowed away beneath all this baggage, and with them the children too small to walk, the feeble old men, the invalids, and those too foot-sore to tramp the weary way.

A delightful picture did I once perceive. Upon the back of a patient donkey numerous tent-poles had been tied; how so small a beast could carry them remains a mystery. Between these poles several small naked babies had been fastened, their black eyes staring at me from beneath mops of tousled, unkempt curls.

The donkey moved from place to place, grazing, the heavy poles bobbed about, one or the other touching the ground, raising little clouds of dust like smoke.

No concern was to be read on the faces of the babies; this mode of transport was no doubt the usual thing. They looked like little brown monkeys brought from warmer climes....

"ON THE BURNING PLAINS OF THE DOBRUDJA WHERE FOR MILES AROUND NO TREE IS TO BE SEEN" (p. 48).

"STIFLED BY THE OVERWHELMING TEMPERATURE, THEY HAD MASSED THEMSELVES TOGETHER" (p. 50).

I have often met old couples wandering together—men and women bent with age, weary, dusty, covered with rags, with pipes in their mouths; wretched vagrants, but always perfectly picturesque. No doubt they were going to tinker in some villages, for the men carried on their backs the inevitable copper pots, whilst the old hags had heavy sacks slung over their shoulders, a thick staff in their hands. Along the sides of their earth-coloured checks grey plaits of hair hung limply down, swinging as they went. It was to me as though I had often met them before; I seemed to recognise their eyes, their weary look, even the shell, sign of the fortune-teller, that the women wore hanging from a string at their girdles; yet no doubt they were but samples of the many wanderers among this people who, homeless and foot-sore, are for ever roaming over the earth....

*

**

One art above all others belongs to the gipsies. They are born musicians, and the violin is their instrument; even the smallest boy will be able to make it sing. Some are musicians by profession. In groups of three and four they will wander from village to village, always where music is needed, patiently, tirelessly playing for hours and hours, in sun or rain, night or day, at marriages, funerals, or on feast-days.

When in bands these wandering minstrels have other instruments besides violins. Strange-shaped lutes, well known in Rumanian literature as the "cobsa," and a flute composed of several reeds, the classical flute used in ages past by old father Pan.

Mostly they are bronze-coloured old vagrants with melancholy eyes and bent backs, who are accustomed to cringe, and whose lean brown hands are accustomed to beg. Discarding their picturesque rags, these wandering minstrels have adopted hideous old clothes that others have cast off. Infinitely more mean-looking are they in this accoutrement; they have lost that indefinite charm that generally surrounds them; they are naught but sad old men clothed in ugly tatters, and are no more a delight to the eyes. Welcome they are, nevertheless, for their music is both sweet and melancholy, strident and weird; there is a strange longing in every note, and the gayer the tunes become the more is one inclined to weep!

An inexplicable cry of yearning lies in their every melody—is it a remembrance of far-off lands that once were theirs, and that they have never seen? Or is it only an expression of the eternal nostalgia that drives them restlessly from place to place?

One summer's evening I met a gipsy youth, coming towards me from out of the dust of the road. Seated with bare, dangling legs on the back of a donkey, his violin under his chin, regardless of all else, he was playing ... playing to the sky above, to the stars that were coming out one by one, peeping down with pale wonder upon this lonely vagabond to whom all the road belonged.... Playing because it was his nature to play ... playing to his heart that had not yet awakened ... playing to his soul that he could not fathom.

*

**

In towns the gipsies are used as masons. One finds them in groups wherever a house is being built, men, women, and children bringing with them their nameless disorder and their picturesque filth.

Of an evening, the work being done, they will prepare their supper, when, seated round the steaming pot, their many-coloured rags become radiant beneath the rays of the setting sun.

Often a mangy donkey is attached not far off, and in a basket, amidst a medley of metal pots of all sizes and shapes, lies a sleeping infant wrapped in a torn cloth.

The donkey patiently bears his burden, flicking away the flies with his meagre tail.

In the month of lilies handsome gipsy-girls will wander through the streets, carrying wooden vessels filled with snow-white flowers, the purity of the lilies strangely in contrast with their sun-tanned faces. In long, fragrant bunches they sell these flowers to the passers-by. At every corner one meets them, either crouching in picturesque attitudes on the pavement or standing upright beneath the shadowy angle of a roof, beautiful creatures with dark faces readily breaking into smiles that make their black eyes glisten and their white teeth flash.

Figures full of unconscious pride, visages at which one must look and always look again ... for they contain all the mystery of the many roads their feet have left behind!

*

**

It is the season of harvest that shows Rumania in all her glory, that season when the labour of man meets its reward, when, the earth having given her utmost, man, woman, and child go forth to gather in the wealth that makes this country what it is.

75

Sometimes, indeed, it is an hour of disappointment, for rain, hail, or drought ofttimes undoes man's weary work. Sometimes the earth has not responded to his dearest hopes, has not been able to bring forth her fruit.

"MOTHERS AND CHILDREN, AND OLD GRANNIES" (p. 53).

"SMALL BRONZE STATUES WITH CURLY, TOUSLED HEADS" (p. 55).

"OCCASIONALLY A TORN SHIRT BARELY COVERS THEM" (p. 55).

"MOST BEAUTIFUL OF ALL ARE THE YOUNG GIRLS" (p. 55).

"INCONCEIVABLY PICTURESQUE" (p. <u>54</u>).

"THESE ARE THE RESPECTED MEMBERS OF THE TRIBES" (p. 54).

"I HAVE OFTEN MET OLD COUPLES WANDERING TOGETHER" (p. 58).

Years have I known when, for months at a time, no drop of rain has fallen, when, like the people of old, we watched the sky in the ardent hope that the cloud as large as a man's hand would spread and burst into the showerso sorely needed—but the cloud passed and gave not the rain it promised; years when all that had been confided to the bosom of the earth withered and dried away because from April to September no drop had fallen, so that numbers of wretched cattle died for want of pasturage upon which to graze.

Terrible months of straining anxiety, of hopeless waiting that seemed to dry up the blood in one's veins, as the earth was parched from the want of rain.

The rivers had no more water; the land of plenty becomes a land of sighs, the dust covering all things as with a shroud of failure....

But grand indeed are the years of plenty, when man's effort bears fruit.

In oceans of ripe gold the corn lies beneath the immense face of the sun, proud of its plenty, a glorious hope fulfilled!

And, from that vast plain of fertility, man's hand it is that reaps the ripe ears, that binds the sheaves, that gathers in the grain. Ever again and again must I marvel at the patience of man's labour, marvel at his extraordinary conquest over the earth.

In groups the peasants work from early dawn to sunset, unaffected by the pulsing heat beating down upon their heads. The men's snowy shirts contrast with the women's coloured aprons that stain the tawny plain with vivid spots of blue, red, or orange, for at the season of harvest no one remains idle—the very old and the disabled alone are left behind to guard the house.

From hour to hour ceaselessly they toil, till midday gathers them round their carts for frugal repast of polenta and onions. Pictures of labour, of healthy effort, of simple content! How often have I contemplated them with emotion, realising how dear this country had grown to my heart.

Watchful dogs guard the carts and those of the children too small to work; beneath the shade of these vehicles the labourers take a short hour's rest, alongside of their grey bullocks that in placid content lie chewing the cud, their enormous horns sending back the rays of the sun. Lazily they swish their tails from side to side, keeping off the too busy flies that gather on their lean flanks and round their large, dreamy eyes. With slow turns of their heads they follow their masters' movements, well aware that their own effort must be taken up again at the hour of sunset when the labourers go home.

Only on rich estates is machinery used, and then mostly for threshing the corn; nearly all the cutting is done by hand. Small gatherings of busy labourers crowd around the iron monster, whose humming voice can be heard from afar, and always rises the heap of grain till it stands, a burnished pyramid of gold, beneath the great blue sky.

At sunset the peasants return home, their scythes over their shoulders, walking beside their carts heaped up with bright yellow straw. Along the road they crawl, those carts, in a haze of dust. On wind-still evenings the dust remains suspended in the air, covering the world with a silvery gauze, enveloping the dying day in a haze of mystery that floats over man and beast, wiping out the horizon, toning down all colours, softening every outline.

Often the sinking sun sets this haze aflame; then the atmosphere becomes strangely luminous, as though a tremendous fire were burning somewhere behind fumes of smoke. Indescribable is that hour; full of beauty, full of peace, full of the infinite satisfaction of work faithfully accomplished, the hour when all feet are turned homewards, turned towards rest.

In never-ending file the carts follow each other, drawn by those grey-white oxen with the wondrous horns—along the road they come as though moving in a dream, that slowly passes in a cloud of dust and is gone; ... but the dust remains suspended like a veil drawn over a vision that is no more....

The maize-harvest comes later in the year, much later; sometimes in October the peasants are still gathering the ripe fruit. The days are short, and in the evening dampness rises out of the vast plain, and hovers like smoke beneath the glowing sky. An indescribable melancholy floats over the world, the melancholy of things come to an end. A great effort seems completed, and now the year has no more to do but to fall slowly to sleep.... Yet nothing is more glorious than the Rumanian autumn; Nature desires to deck herself in a last mantle of beauty before confessing herself vanquished by the advancing of the winter season.

The sky becomes intensely blue; all that stands up against it appears to acquire a new value. The trees dress themselves in wondrous colours, sometimes golden, sometimes russet, sometimes flaming red. Amongst the man-high maize-plants, giant sunflowers stand bending their heads, heavy with the weight of the seeded centres; like prodigious stars their saffron petals shine against the azure vault.

Whole fields have I seen of these giant plants, real armies of sun-shaped flowers, triumphantly yellow beneath the rays of the great light they so bravely mimic. But often it seems to me that ashamedly they turn their faces away, sadly aware that they are but a sorry imitation of the one whose name they bear. Oil is made out of the seeds of these flowers; therefore do the peasants cultivate them in such numbers.

Often beneath the shade of those giant plants have I seen peasants seated in circles round piles of maize, separating the fruit from the leaves. In dwarf pyramids of orange, the ripe cobs lie scattered about the wilting fields, their glorious colour attracting the eye from afar; often the women's kerchiefs are of the very same tint.

"A BARE FIELD WHERE THE SOLDIERS EXERCISED"

I love these flaming touches of colour amongst the arid immensities of reaped fields—lovingly the eye of the artist lingers to look at them, only unwillingly turning away.

A pretty sight is also that of the peasant meetings, either in large barns or courtyards, to unsheathe the grain of maize from its cob. These are occasions of great rejoicing, when the young folk flock together, when laughter and work mingle joyously, when long yarns are told and love-songs are sung. The old crones sit around spinning or weaving, their heads nodding together over delectable gossip, one eye upon the youths and maidens, who, dressed in their brightest, with a flaring flower stuck behind the ear, ogle each other, and joke and kiss and are happy.

The old gipsy "Lautar," or wander-minstrel, is never absent from these meetings. From somewhere he is sure to come limping along, shabby, disreputable, a sordid figure with his violin or his "cobsa" under his arm; but his music is wonderful, making all hearts laugh, or dance, or weep.

*

**

Too many pictures would I evoke, too many visions rise before my brain—both time and talent fail me—so grudgingly must I turn away and leave these simple people to their work and their play, to their joys and their pains, their hopes and their fears. I leave them to their peaceful homes—a veil of dust lying over.

THE END

POSTSCRIPT

Rumania, like the other small nations, is paying a bloody price for her vindication of the principles of Right—the bedrock of the Allied cause.

Her plucky intervention in the Great War, notwithstanding what had befallen Belgium, Serbia and Montenegro; the implicit faith of her people in the righteousness of the Allied cause; and the gallantry of her troops excite the admiration of all the Free Races.

The British Red Cross Society and Order of St. John has rendered great assistance on the battlefields of Rumania with hospitals well staffed and medical supplies.

We owe a debt to Rumania. Every copy of My Country sold adds to *The Times* Fund for Sick and Wounded, for which purpose this tribute by Queen Marie to the little-known natural and architectural beauties of her country is published. Should any reader, as a result of this book, desire to send a further contribution, this may be addressed to the publishers, Messrs. Hodder & Stoughton, St. Paul's House, Warwick Square, London, E.C., *marked* My Country, and will be duly acknowledged in the columns of *The Times*.

December 1916.

CPSIA information can be obtained at www.ICGtesting.com
Printed in the USA
LVOW04s1626010515

436906LV00011B/605/P